THE FORTUNE
500 BEND
IN TIME RESEARCH PROJECT

A NOVELLA

RICHARD A. BOEHLER, JR.

authorHOUSE®

AuthorHouse™
1663 Liberty Drive
Bloomington, IN 47403
www.authorhouse.com
Phone: 833-262-8899

Published by AuthorHouse 09/22/2022

ISBN: 978-1-6655-7134-0 (sc)
ISBN: 978-1-6655-7133-3 (e)

Print information available on the last page.

This book is printed on acid-free paper.

CONTENTS

Acknowledgements ix

Chapter 1 1
Chapter 2 61
Chapter 3 116

Acknowledgements

- **To the All-American University** – for a good foundation in writing, reading and science.

- **To lost love:** where would we be without some heart ache? What was lost helps us understand, provides a deeper sense of patience and appreciation for future love....

- **To the United States Navy** (active and reserve training opportunities).

- **To all authors** that inspire us to read and some to read and write: Michael Crighton, Stephen King, Stephanie Myer....

- **To my children,** who inspire me to see that there is hope for the future....

CHAPTER 1

The company was located deep in the mountains of northern New Jersey. A perfect place to conduct a variety of secret experiments. Cutoff from the public, the campus was surrounded by sharp ridged mountainous forests. Randy was a research scientist for a large pharmaceutical company. The company employed 70,000 people, around the world. The headquarters was based in Basel, Switzerland. Its New Jersey facility was the largest plant in the United States. The grounds of the NJ complex was the size of two large University campuses. Each day, very early in the morning [before sunrise], Randy would leave his modest Suffolk

County home and travel the stretch of the Long Island expressway. The LIE was about a forty-minute drive west from eastern Long Island [farm country], to the lights of New York City. The lights never grew old to Randy. Each morning, he zoomed through the NYC theater district as he absorbed the energy of the many bright "time square area" lights! It was refreshing to his soul. It was something that really could not be described accurately with words. It was more of a feeling. The transfer of city life energy into his veins. It's not that he did not feel fatigued. Some mornings were tougher than other mornings. The caffeine from the coffee helped him with the start of each commute. And, as he approached the lights from the city.... the energy propelled Randy right through the Lincoln tunnel, into northern New Jersey. After reaching the garden state, the rest of the commute was a breeze. Most people were travelling into the city for their morning commute. Not as many people travelled up north, deep into the desolate northern New Jersey mountains!

So why would Randy want to be part of a small group of drivers, heading north five days a week? It was the company. It was the project. It encompassed many "research pillars" that were built, through time. The pillars were for the pursuit of excellence. A pursuit of innovative science. A pursuit of knowledge and eventually a dose of wisdom. His studies started in a small town, 20 minutes south of the research facility. He had read about large production of the chemical "agent orange". Large stock piles were being produced in the late 1960s and 1970s, to support the war efforts in Vietnam. When the war ended the production of agent orange stopped. The government sealed the entire area with columns and slabs of cement... and did not do a good job of it. The word "seal" should have been used loosely. It was more of a sloppy covering to the deadly agent, the "agent orange".

In the early evenings, twice a week.... Randy would park his car on the side of the river banks, near the old agent orange production facility. He would do this just prior to heading back to Long Island for the night. Randy started collecting soil and water samples on the side walls of the river.... The samples were representative of the environment that was located downstream from agent orange production areas....

It was a good start to a "hot research topic". He enjoyed the studies and brought the samples to his "mountain" lab for analysis. What he didn't realize [at the time the one agent orange project started] was what he would later stumble upon.... A discovery that would reveal something so fascinating, so enlightening to the human realm of curiosity. Deep in the mountain, Randy travelled along a narrow road. The road was cut right through the rock. Eventually he reached the guard shack of the mountainous research facility. The company facility was surrounded, not only by the trees... but, also by an iron perimeter fence. At the guard shack, Randy showed his identification for electronic scan. This checked him into the facility. It also kept track of his work hours. Within the facility gates were many buildings. Each building was dedicated to a separate and different research project. The central building had a day care facility in it. Randy did not have kids, but realized that the day care existed because the food court was also located in the same building.

Most mornings he would stop at the central building to pick up the local newspaper and eat a large cup of oatmeal. He would add fresh fruit to the oatmeal... an attempt to maintain a healthy diet. The coffee was good, the food selection was phenomenal and it was nice to sit at a restaurant style table. It was early, around six AM. His shift didn't start till seven thirty. So, he had time to read through the NJ "record" newspaper.... The café was typically empty, that early in the morning. Most people lived quite locally to the mountain research facility. Locally, meaning that it took twenty to thirty minutes to commute. His colleagues lived in New Jersey or the Rockland New York mountain area.

Randy had a much longer drive, coming all the way from Long Island. He did not mind though. There were certainly mornings that were more challenging than others.... but, he did like to drive the length of Long Island – through Suffolk county, then through Nassau county. Then arriving in the Long Island City area (Queens, where he was born). There was familiarity in the Queens area. Even though he had moved out onto the Long Island farm country when he was five years old.... He still continued to drive into queens as often as possible to visit family. His parents did not continue to visit the family much in Queens. Sadly, this happens all to often. They just lost touch with the family. Randy was happy to drive his car into queens and visit his grand-parents... on his mother's side. Mostly Polish, with some German roots. The trip was always an adventure. A fresh start each day. A fresh start to work on new research projects. At the New Jersey research facility.... Randy walked along the path, outside the central building – He abruptly stumbled upon a visitor. He felt he had been followed.... The feeling that one gets as a stalker stares at its victim..., this visitor was not human. The garden state of New Jersey is so beautiful. It truly is the "garden state", with a bloom of pretty plant flowers. Historically looking, large oak trees (and many other tree types). A canopy of "rain forest-like" green tree tops. But, the visitor that followed Randy was approaching quickly and swiftly. The visitor was a beautiful NJ hawk! These birds are majestic! They circle the NJ sky with incredible wing spans. Randy was used to this visitor though! He would see this visitor most early mornings. The same visitor was present in the evenings, as he headed home. Randy believed in the after-life....

Randy believed that a "spirit", the transfer of energy made its way to other places in time. The energy was also transferred into these great majestic birds! That was just a theory though. Maybe more than a theory... It was just something he knew. He felt this "knowledge of energy transfer" deep within his own soul. Deep within his own spirit. It was a gift, or a curse (depending on how one looked at it). The Catholic religion never taught Randy to believe in "energy transfer". In fact, the teachings of his faith were completely opposite. There was no "reincarnation". It was a one-way ticket to the pearly white gates. Randy thought, well that could be true. But, why not a remanence of partial energy that surrounded the human soul... or perhaps a remanence of the soul itself? He was curious, always interested in this since he felt things and remembered events from other places... events from other points in time.... This was not common to all.... But, he was sure that there were others with this gift.... With this curse. More than just familiarity, it was serendipity? De ja vu? The good, and sometimes the not so good... the tragic end of a life... and that was perhaps it. An abrupt tragic end of a life in the past was transferred directly into a baby.... Not so far-fetched, was it? It was a dog fight. The war was most likely World War II. He recalls the face of the Japanese fighter pilot bearing in on him. Abruptly firing his airplane cannons... The life of a United States pilot ended during that aggressive air fight.... The energy transferred to elsewhere and with it.... The remnants of a strong drink at a night club with his love... In the "new life", the creator of such complexity and awesome energy made sure that Randy would have a love of airplanes... but, also an incredible fear to leave the ground, with terrible ocular depth perception....

Randy enjoyed the morning air. It was fresh, it was crisp. He was happiest early in the morning. As Randy often drove through the campus gates and entered the narrow roadway, he would think about how that great hawk lived. Randy often observed the bird, with incredible wing span, fly through the sky. The New Jersey hawk circled gracefully and gently.... In search of prey, perhaps. Or maybe just enjoyed the scenery up above. Randy felt a connection with this bird. Early each morning, the bird was spotted on top of the largest building. And, most evenings the bird was in the sky, circling....It was a typical day in the research realm. The laboratory was located in the basement of a large twenty story marble building. It was quite grand, with incredible architecture. The building was one of many, evenly spaced throughout the gated grounds. The process just to get into the research project was very competitive. It started with a telephone conversation, which led to a follow up teleconference. In the teleconference there were five different area leads [that he was aware of during the long 3-hour interview]. Randy liked it. What was presented in the teleconference. It was not easy stuff. Science rarely is simple. It encompasses multiple steps, based on theory – with practical application. The committee was probing potential candidates. Randy passed this process and was invited on campus, a month later, for the conference room interview. The campus interview was longer and tougher! There he met many great people and was happy to get the news of a start date! The research area had many different projects in the pipeline. Randy was able to work through the projects…. The current project was a biological science study.

The environment in an area where agent orange was manufactured was contaminated. The river that ran through the mountain town was the Hudson. Enormous and fierce in some areas. And in other areas, the river was calm. Randy had soil samples from the side of the town's river banks in cold storage. As he got the tools of science ready... he walked toward the cold storage room, lost in thought. He was thinking about the area of the river bank that he got the soil sample from... After parking his car, some distance from the water, he hiked toward the river. Randy did not realize at the time that there was an enormous drop, near the river's edge... He almost fell down the river bank! Fortunately, he caught a large tree root.

The tree saved him from plummeting down about fifty feet, into the raging river! As Randy entered the cold storage room, he checked the temperature charts to ensure that the optimal temperature had been maintained. The goal was to keep any microbes "alive" (viable). After removing the soil samples from cold storage, he let the samples warm to ambient (room) temperature. This was a standard approach in the area of "environmental microbiology". He was a full-time scientist by day, and enrolled in some part-time doctorate classes during the evening. His specialty was microbiology. The applications in the environment (in air, in soil, in water, etc.) were his novel skill goals. The University program in NJ was good. It was a continuation of the foundations he had earned in previous curriculum (at the biological sciences, bachelor level and at the microbiology/ immunology graduate level). The soil samples were now ready for testing... There was something strange with these soil samples. Randy had anticipated that the soil would be full of ATP (an energy marker). The samples were mostly "dead". The microbes had been killed by something. Measurements of energy (ATP) were small to almost null (no detection). He documented all the results in a standard lab notebook and began to transfer the raw data to excel spread sheets. This was a good tool to collect and organize large amounts of raw data, with the ultimate goal to sift through it....to make sense of it.... To statistically trend it.... There were little to no trends, the soil was "dead". Randy did not understand how this could be, since the raging Hudson river was full of life-giving water!

Re-visit to the 50-foot Hudson River Bank Cliff

He parked his car across the street. The raging Hudson river was fierce during his visit. Randy was hungry for dinner. But, would wait until he returned to his modest suburban Long Island house. His wife, Cheryl, would be waiting for him. Most nights she had a wonderful dinner ready. Not because she had too, not because Randy expected it. It was more of a mutual understanding for one another. They enjoyed eating a late dinner together. She was an executive for a local pharmaceutical company. Her expertise was new drugs, that were coming to market. She traveled approximately 15 to 20%, throughout the year. Randy thought about the diner selection tonight... It was probably "Chinese" food. They often shared shredded bamboo shoots, with hunan beef – on Mondays. The Hudson river was unusually high this Monday evening. Randy was careful to walk along side the river bank. In the distance, upstream from where he was located – he noticed a large antique looking building... It seemed abandoned. The building was probably part of the agent orange operation. Instead of collecting samples, Randy decided to leave the river bank and explore the distant structure. The sun was setting in the western sky. There would not be much time, before the sunlight disappeared... Randy did not have much supplies with him. He did have a basic flash light. Which would certainly help with a dark situation... At the entrance of the old building was a rusted, broken iron gate. The gate had a chain and pad lock on it. He easily passed through the gate and followed a grass/weeded pathway to the front door. Inside the building, Randy noticed something odd. The part of the floor, in front of a large stair case had been removed. A dark hole in the floor was observed. He wondered where this could lead to? But, the sun was just about to set in the distant sky behind him. It was time to head home.

The drive back to "Long Island" was smooth. Not too much traffic on the roadways at seven. Rush hour was more between four and six in the evenings. Any time after that was a breeze for Randy. The trip between northern new jersey and eastern Suffolk long island was approximately one hour and forty minutes. Approaching nine in the evening, Randy was welcomed home by his newly wed wife Cheryl.

It was dark and she was glowing a fluorescent light green! Her pajamas were soft cotton white, with UFO's, flying saucers... it was a cute style... she loved the government conspiracy theories of "Area 51".... Her selection of night clothes was inviting... soft, subtle, with a hint of sensuality...lots of skin....

They shared something special. The relationship blossomed from a friendship – the best relationships often do. This was different though. There were unspoken connections between Cheryl and Randy. [Randy supposed he could attribute these connections to Cheryl's "conspiracy theories". It was really not too far fetched though]. There was a mutual understanding of one another. A biological connection through "unseen pheromones". A like-minded interest in some, but not all activities. God knows, Randy would not want to have two of his personality running around! She was gentle most of the time, and soft spoken. Unique in her styles... he loved that. Genuine in her nature – and had a tendency to get angry at times....with justifiable reasoning.... He loved that about her too! She was aggressive when she needed to be.... And gentle the rest of the time... A unique personality, for sure!They enjoyed dinner together. Cheryl enlightened Randy of the unusual "object" that crashed into a near by long island park. It was late at night, a few weeks back... the government came in and quarantined the surrounding area... Randy smiled at her and asked "are you sure it was the government that came in a did that?" She looked angry, then smiled. A large government truck came in and removed a large metal object from the area! I have pictures! Randy believed her. He then shared his findings in the antique production facility. Cheryl was intrigued. I'm not sure why in the world there is a piece of the floor missing, at the base of the stair well.... Cheryl stopped him. Let's find out! They agreed to return to the NJ river bank early Saturday, they would take the train in to New Jersey state. The train was located just next to their home. The house was modest and on a small piece of property. They loved it! It had a washer and dryer. Although, to conserve energy, there were many times when Cheryl would hang damp washed clothes on a "clothes line". There were actually two lines. One located outside, in the backyard. The other line was located right in the warm laundry room.

Before the trip into New Jersey, they rested and had light conversation. The conversation was interesting to Randy. Cheryl continued her assumptions about little green men, flying saucers and a recent crash in the local park. She believed that there was more to the story. It just did not add up. Why would the government come into a local Long Island park and "rope it off"? The cautionary tape was bright yellow and in large print was "DO NOT ENTER". Randy smiled at Cheryl. She was cute, with her conspiracy theories. He asked how she knew all this? Of course, she was shy to admit that her and her friends had visited the park... in search for UFOs! The stories fascinated Randy. He hoped she did not run into the mother ship, where they would take her away to another place... He was giggling and truly did enjoy her active creativity. Perhaps, there was something to her conspiracies. Perhaps, they were not just conspiracies. Who knew? In any event, what Randy was about to present to Cheryl, would certainly blow her mind! It was much more factual. His findings in the deserted antique style New Jersey house would fascinate her. He was thinking how to start, but did not have much of a chance to "prepare" for the "ice breaker story of a life-time"! Cheryl could see the subtle thinker, in motion... sort of like "poetry in motion!". Randy advised his lover that the house they were traveling to was empty, with some strangeness to it. Randy not only found a floor entrance that led down to a dark stair-cased abyss. The stairs seemed easy to follow, as long a they travelled carefully with flash lights. It was what he found in the house that sparked his curious mind. Cheryl listened CLOSELY to Randy, as he provided the details of alien- like wall writings, a luminescent yellowish glow along the deep stair wall, the shape of the hand prints.... These hand prints did not represent a five fingered human hand print. There were only three fingers! The creature that left the hand print on the walls must have been moist, excreting some kind of glowing liquid from where the hands touched the walls!

It was early Saturday morning. They had stopped at a local coffee shop for fresh liquid caffeine, and bagels. The train station was literally within walking distance from the modest suburban home. A home they had come to love. It was what was inside the home that they grew to love. They filled the walls with modern styled art. They filled hallways with impressionistic style art. And what wall space was left... they added photos from various road trips, over many years together... After a quick breakfast, they made their way home to park the car and walk to the train station. The station was not a "direct route" train line. And that was good, since the trains rarely traveled the tracks past their home. The main rail line was about twenty minutes south of their town, in a place called "Patchogue, Long Island". The main rail line came from New York City, and traveled across Long Island – past Patchogue, right to the end (near Montauk point). On the train, Cheryl listened to Randy elaborate on the river bank facility. There was something really strange about that facility. The property was abandoned. It had been desolate; from when the Vietnam War ended in the 1970s... That's fifty + years! There was much more to the facility. Entry was easy enough. However, inside Randy noticed that there was no electricity. He tried some of the wall switches. That made sense. At the back center of a large lobby was a huge marble stair case. Above was a hanging light fixture – very fancy. Gold plated, with crystal. Lots of dust though. Randy wanted to start climbing the stairs, but was quickly stopped with the observance of a gapping hole in the floor. Located right in front of the first step.

Cheryl interrupted – "so what are we talking about here? Extra terrestrial findings? Unidentified Objects? Little green men?" She smiled. More of a smirk, with an incredible cuteness!

Randy did not know, but they would find out. And as the train entered Manhattan, they made their way to the subway system. A quick subway ride to the bus terminal took only about twenty minutes. The bus terminal was located just next to the Lincoln Tunnel. They needed to decide how to make their way to the river bank. The bus would drop them off at a local New Jersey town. From there, they would need to catch a ride. They chose the taxi route. Just before the exiting of the taxi cab, they went through their school back pack of supplies. They had some water, a few protein bars. Two good flash lights, and a fluorescent chalk marker – used to mark the dark halls, as they traveled into the unknown facility. Randy paid the taxi fare and there they stood, just next to the cliff – overlooking a turbulent

Hudson river. Something fierce this Saturday, since the moon was full – and a storm was approaching. The sky opened to pellet sized hail, gusty wind, lightning followed with rumbles of thunder. They quickly walked the path, through the rusty gates and to the front doors of the facility....

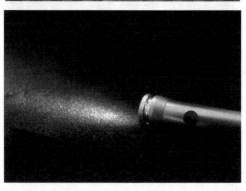

Into the Dark Abyss

Cheryl pulled the two flash lights from her back pack. The lights were very good, providing a strong beam of light. They entered the front doors and immediately found the marble stair case. The facility was impressive. As Randy had presented to Cheryl, there they found the hole in the lobby floor. It wasn't that the hole was there by accident. It seemed to have been hidden at one time. Looking closely at the edge of the hole, Cheryl pointed to a hidden sliding panel. The panel could be pulled across the floor, to completely cover the dark space. They moved forward, and followed the beam of light from the flashlight. There was a simple set of stairs, descending into the floor.

Within a matter of fifteen to twenty minutes, the steps ended. The light revealed a long, spacious platform. At the one end of the "room" was some sort of clear plexiglass. At the other end of the room was a large book case, with a display of prominent titled literature. Just beside the book shelf were a few chairs and a round table. It was a lobby! An underground lobby. For what, they did not know.... Not yet. As Cheryl and Randy opened discussion about their next "move", the distant sound of a railway car approaching was heard. The plexiglass doors quickly opened! Cheryl reacted by grabbing Randy and darting across the room, to hide behind the large wooden book case. They were able to see through the stack of books, into the empty lobby/room....

Two people exited a "car-like" shuttle and entered the lobby. As they passed the book case, it was obvious that some human qualities were not there! They looked human from a distance, but up close it was apparent that the facial features were more "flattened". For example, the bridge of the nose was missing! There were just two slits for breathing air? The eyes were much larger than a typical human eye ball! And in the dark, the faint (but steady) glow of a green-yellow luminescence was observed! Randy and Cheryl did not dare speak until the glow ascended up the stairs and enough time had passed.The shuttle seemed simple enough, the ride would follow a track (similar to a train) into a large clear tube. There were four rows of seats, offering plenty of space for at least eight passengers. Cheryl did not notice too much computer guidance within the shuttle. It seemed to have a "switch" that just toggled in the forward direction. This would start the initiation sequence. Cheryl asked Randy if he was ready to travel into the unknown? He smiled with a firm nod yes! The toggle switch was gently moved into the forward position, which was followed by the shuttle door closing. After the door entrance door released a noticeable air pressure sound, the car rolled quietly along the tracks. The speed was moving at a moderate thirty to forty miles per hour. At least that was what the gauge read. The railway tube that they were guiding along in must have been pressurized, since they did not feel any popping of the ear drums.

As the car dove deep into the tunnel, which led out into open ocean... there were signs that gave some clue to their orientation... the distance traveled and their destination. The only stop was deep into the ocean abyss. A place near the ocean depths, called "the bend in time research facility"Cheryl was wearing an adventurous jump suit. Perfect for the travel. Her beige suit was complemented with timberland work boots. To complete the look, she scrunched her long blonde hair in a pony tail. Randy wore beige shorts, a black tank top with matching timberland work boots. His ball cap was black with the red New Jersey hockey team mascot on it!

They could not believe that they decided to move forward with exploration into the dark abyss. It was sort of a sense of "manifest destiny". An inner curiosity that needed to be filled. Randy enjoyed the talk, as the shuttle continued to slowly descend deep into the ocean water. They could see out into the ocean. Not that it was clear water. But a light was present, just outside the car. Perhaps the lighting was attached to the inner wall of the clear tube. The tube that surrounded the rail and shuttle. Amazing technology. Although, the transport had an "antique" feel to it. As if it had been around, in the deep ocean for quite some time.... Hundreds of years? Thousands of years? Perhaps, a hundred thousand years? They did not know. They had the feeling that they would certainly find out!

The shuttle moved slowly and gently, along the tracks. It was approaching a "docking station". And eventually came to a complete stop. A voice was suddenly heard – the docking was momentary. The purpose was to equilibrate the pressure, before continuing to dive deeper along the tracks. Randy suggested that it was probably just a safety mechanism. Since the surrounding tube was already "pressurized" and did not change much as they descended. He was watching the dash board gauges, as they traveled deep into the ocean. The interior car pressure remained neutral, with little change. The outer pressure gauge showed some fluctuation... but, not too significant. That was his extrapolation and understanding for the surrounding tube having a constant pressure.

As they left the docking station, Cheryl felt a strange sensation. She asked Randy if he felt as if someone or something was "watching them". The lights flickered then went suddenly dark. Cheryl screamed! The lights came back on. She grabbed her back-shoulder blade and said that something bit her! Randy looked at her bare skin, but did not see much of anything. Except for a pink area of irritation. A small zone. He laughed and said, maybe the aliens injected you with a high-tech Unidentified Tracking Device! She did not share his humor.As the shuttle made its way further into the abyss, they could see a large ship. What looked like an enormous round space ship ... may-be that was just the design of the underground facility. It was like a floating city. Just, under water – deep in the Atlantic Ocean, somewhere off the coast of New Jersey....

The Under-Water Research Facility

So, just like that – they were docked under many miles of salty oceanic water. After making what seemed to be about ten stops (to equilibrate pressure, or perhaps just the design of the safety mechanisms for under water travel...) they were submerged into the dark abyss. Funny thing, though, they were more excited. For one thing, the darkness was not so dark. They were surrounded, as they could see through the clear shuttle tube, with a very pretty yellow-green bioluminescent glow. The light followed the edges of the underwater facility, it also followed the surrounding storage shed. And as they looked out, in aw, they observed sea life. Fish, and larger sea creatures swimming around. These sea creatures all exhibited a brilliant luminescent glow! The shuttle door abruptly opened. Cheryl and Randy were startled, as their focus had been directed outside – in the glowing abyss.

They were greeted by Professor Elof. A heavy set man, with a jolly smile. His facial features were of an emeritus life-long professor (which he was). He had white to grey hair, a beard and thick glasses. He introduced himself and quickly followed with: "what in the world are you two doing down here?" Come, get out of the car and let's go to the dining quarter; a place to get a hot cup of coffee and a meal. Cheryl and Randy followed – hand in hand, together [they were always together, soul mates....].

The facility was enormous! With modern style art design. However, in the dining quarter, there was a shift to "antique style". A more homely feel to the area. The walls were etched in what appeared to be golden style trim. Followed with dark cherry wood furniture. Inside some of the furniture, they could see china plates, crystal glasses, etc. There, they were greeted by a young research assistant – Tina. She too was jolly – and very happy to see Cheryl and Randy. Tina was in her early 20s – and explained the research goals of the facility. That sparked an immediate flash of interest to Randy and Cheryl! They were curious about the facility – how long had it been in this area? Why was it so secret? Tina went on to give a brief presentation of the facilities history. She did not sugar coat it. The facility was not a human made design. They were, in fact, having a meal – with hot coffee – in a UFO! The unidentified ship had come to the ocean thousands of years earlier.... There were no survivors, something had happened.... Tina went on to say that the real crux of it was: "the technology they found in this mother ship...!"

As they were eating a delicious hot cooked meal, Cheryl looked down the adjacent hall. She observed what looked like a black cat. Only thing was that it had a curious glow to its eyes. The size of the creature was much larger than a typical cat. Randy asked Cheryl if she was okay? She smiled, and they continued to listen to Tina talk about the research facilities rich history. Cheryl was suddenly startled by the abrupt presence of the same black cat – right next to her! [she thought to herself, how in the world did this creature travel from the hall into the dining area so quickly?]. Tina stopped her presentation and giggled. Sorry for the entrance of the cat.... She is a bit of a mystery. We found her, right on this ship – when we started working here! The cat seemed to grin, not a friendly grin.... The grin was more of a sinister horrific smile toward Cheryl. Cheryl snuggled closer to Randy. There were many people working in the research facility. It literally was a "floating city", housing approximately 5,000 people! There were living quarters, dining quarters (similar to the dining area they were currently in), recreational areas, movie houses, and even a McDonalds!

Professor Elof returned to ask if Cheryl and Randy would like to stay the weekend? They replied with an enthusiastic "Yes"! Tina showed the two to their sleeping area and were given fresh blankets and pillow cases. The first night was very peaceful, they enjoy the antique styled room. It had all the comfort of a nice hotel room. The room had a small coffee pot, which Randy was quick to brew. During that short time of "coffee brewing", Cheryl slipped into something more comfortable. Randy sipped his fresh coffee, turned around to a surprise! Cheryl was wearing soft white pajamas. He loved her style. Sometimes, she would find the perfect moment to turn an ordinary evening into "pure love". Randy adored the way she was able to calm him. She asked for a cup of coffee, and they joined each other on the bed. The air was cool, from a very effective air conditioner. The television was "high tech". There were selections of movies and many different channels. Cheryl found her interest – the UFO sci-fi channel! Randy jumped in the bathroom for a quick shower, and returned sporting boxer shorts and no shirt. The coffee warmed him. But, it was the unspoken aura of love that truly warmed any chills that he might have had from the cool room air.Her long blond hair was soft and silky, with a vanilla aroma... fascinating, Randy never understood how a lady could keep such a sweet aroma in her hair.... And, it seemed to flourish from all of her skin. The sweetest scent the senses could feel, could smell, could taste. They fell asleep, as the brewed coffee stayed fresh in the coffee pot thermal apparatus....

A visit to the engineering levels

There were literally thousands of people around the facility. And as Tina brought Cheryl and Randy to the engineering deck, she was excited to start a discussion about natural resources. Tina advised that the main ships power was a fusion reactor – fascinating, nuclear power. The crew would wear a small piece of a tool on their arm. It measured radiation levels. Most would not be exposed to much. Not more that your typical x-rays that were encountered through out normal life spans... They arrived at what looked like a giant "green-house". It was beautiful and amazing. All the flowers, plants, and even trees the eye could see. Right away Randy noticed the oak, pine and white birch trees. They were outstanding! There was a natural lake in the center of the room, the center of the lab? Was it a large lab? Basically, it was a living and breathing green-house that generated oxygen for the ship. The air was effectively distributed through the ships ventilation system....

The three walked through the green brush and colorful mini-forest! After the tour of this area, Tina asked if the two would be interested in swimming? They all agreed to meet in another level of the ship, where they would exit. After exiting the ship safely, the three would swim to a "docking area". The docking area had an indoor swim area. The ocean, with a bubble of air on top of it – around it... The abyss was dark, yet the luminescence that surrounded them provided a good light source. Inside the large lake style "pool", the three met a few more workers. They enjoyed swimming together. After a few hours, most people left the area. The ones that remained were Tina, Randy and Cheryl. Tina proposed a game! The game was sort of a "tag game". At one end of the pool, Cheryl quickly swam to. The other end, Randy swam to. Tina hid near the outskirts of the lake. The object of the game was to swim from one end to the other, back and forth or which ever direction Cheryl and Randy wanted to swim…. Tina was the "shark". She would only be able to tag them if they were off of the "bases". The bases were at each end of the pool and at a small dock, located in the near center part of the pool. They played this game for what seemed hours! It was fun! The three enjoyed tagging and near misses. It was Randy's turn to be the shark…. Most of the abyss ocean water was dark. There were some glows within the water…. This added to the mystery of the water game. And as the players swam from one end of the pool to the next area, the darkness created a brief "fear" and rush of adrenaline! Randy was approaching the next player for a tag, he thought. He reached out to grab and or just tap gently.... Nothing but water? He was sure that he saw swimming and movement directly in front of him.... It was dark, and then he heard the two female voices in the distance. Suddenly, a dark cat like shadow swam quickly around him... and then... directly in front of him and a sinister glow of animal eyes was observed.... There was no chance to swim away from it, as large fangs ripped into his shoulder blade!Luckily the girls were not too far from Randy, and heard a snarl. They brought him back to the main ship. He woke in the dining room, to a pretty living room fire place (hologram)....

They were getting hungry, and dinner was approaching on a Saturday evening. Randy was thinking that the weekend went by to fast. Professor

Elof met with everyone in the living room area. A movie was playing, the fire place was not burning real wood. However, a good amount of heat was being ventilated into the room. The food was brought out on portable tables and enjoyed by the group of researchers. The professor asked if Cheryl was enjoying her stay on the ship. She smiled and agreed, it was an amazing adventure – and wished that they could stay longer. The professor was oddly quiet and had a look of fear in his face. Finally, the professor was prompted by an incoming colleague to advise everyone of an "accident". A tragic accident had occurred on the ship. One researcher had died! And, as part of the protocol for such "accidents" the ship would be on "lock-down" for fifteen days. During that time, there would be no travel from the ship, through the transport car – back to the surface!

The details were not given at that moment. But, there were "meetings" scheduled for updates…. And the group was advised of an increase in the security patrols, especially during the night hours. With that, the professor wished all a good night – and departed for his office, or maybe his bedroom…. A few of the researchers, including Tina, Randy and Cheryl stayed to eat desert and watch some movies! They were disturbed to hear of the tragic news. But, since there were little details of what actually happened – they did not seem to think "worrying" would help the situation. Tina asked Cheryl if they wanted to see some things tomorrow…as she was rudely interrupted by Randy! "Don't you know movie etiquette?" NO

TALKING DURING THE MOVIE! Tina did not know Randy that well, and was taken by surprise. Cheryl nudged her.... He is just kidding, "a dry odd sense of humor with this one!". They laughed and Randy came over to Cheryl to start tickling her! She was laughing harder. Randy asked if Tina was ticklish too? He grabbed her foot and caused additional laughter in the room. Some of the other researchers laughed. But there were a few that did not care for the humor! So, they stopped and continued to watch the movie together. The next day Tina would introduce Cheryl and Randy to incredible technology. She called it "alien technology". And that is exactly what it was! Technology from out of this world. They had a grasp on some of the workings of these technological breakthroughs. And the areas of technology that they did not fully understand... well, that was one of the main reasons for the 5,000 crew of researchers on the ship. Each research group had specialties. Some were gurus of biological sciences. Others were experts in the field of physical science. Quantum physics was a big area of research....

Deck 5: The Second Murder

They were walking down a dark, narrow, hallway together. Cheryl and Randy noticed some dimly lit fixtures at the top of the ceiling... On any other night, they would have thought the scenery to be kind of "romantic". But, not tonight. They had left the living room entertainment in search of the kitchen. Randy wanted some snacks! And Cheryl was up for some "exploration". As they walked slowly down the corridor, together. Cheryl led the way. They held hands as they took steps toward the kitchen. What they thought was the direction of the "kitchen". Cheryl was quiet and she was a good guide... she was always a good navigator of direction. Randy followed, and as he held her hand he drifted into a cool winters evening, not too long ago. Cheryl had offered to babysit at a family home, on a Friday evening. Randy was excited to meet her there. He drove to the home, on a dark cold evening – last winter. The previous week pelted the landscape with a powerful winter storm. Almost a foot of snow and ice had fallen! It was the storm of the century! Or, at least, the biggest storm that season!

Randy carried his football with him that night. He did not know why. It was kind of stupid, actually. But, not to him. It was more of a "symbol"; the symbol of the "football pigskin!". He was fatigued from a long day of classes. This was before Cheryl and Randy left high school.... Some time ago.... Perhaps it was the setting of the "cold winter's night", or perhaps it was the fact that a "storm had swept through the area". He did not know for sure why he kept this sort of "memory locked away"? Perhaps it was just a reason that he would never fully understand.... A divine situation? Cheryl grabbed Randy's hand and squeezed: "are you okay?". He replied: "okay dokey!" And he was. He was content, happy.... With the warm feeling, as if he finished a few glasses of rum – in a sailor's bar! They continued to walk slowly down the dark corridor.... And Randy again drifted into the memory.... He entered her families' home... She was all smiles, from ear to ear! The kids are in bed, upstairs! Randy smiled back. Lets just go outside for a few minutes. I want to show you something. They did not leave the house for long and they left the door open, so they could hear if the kids woke. Randy brought his football. It was very dark, icy, with hills of snow. He asked if Cheryl could go about ten yards across the yard. She did. He tossed the football at her, gently. She caught it and said: "now what". He smiled, and paused. This is a "tackling drill!". She laughed: Are you serious? And he was. Randy asked Cheryl to throw the ball at him. And after he caught it, he would run across the yard.... Directly at her! And, she would... tackle him! They did this for a good amount of time. Changing the roles of the tackler and the ball carrier.

They slid all over the iced terrain and she was surprisingly a great tackler! Some snow flakes fell calmly in the crisp night air, and they eventually returned to the home. Inside they warmed to cups of hot chocolate... and changed their clothes. Garth Brooks was playing on the living room stereo... a great country singer they loved... and had been happy to have seen live in concert! Cheryl stopped Randy and said "there it is! The kitchen!".

The kitchen was of modern style. Very classy and trimmed with antique dark wood. There was art there. Architecture of the "ship" was incredible! Randy had hoped that there were at least some ring dings in this incredible facility! They giggled....Just above the kitchen area was the next level of the "space ship". It was a large open spaced area. Similar to a bridge or control area, where engineers kept travel coordination. The area was dimly lit when a couple came wondering in. They were scientists recently engaged. A small city, under water. That is where they were. Who knew? What an incredible find! The couple were talking about how fascinating the ship was…. They had just started working in one of the secret research areas, one month ago. The dimly lit surrounding were perfect settings for what made its way toward the couple. It was a shadow figured person. What seemed to be a person, that had little facial features. The couple tried to greet the approaching figure, but it was too late! The swift figure swept extremely fast and aggressively into the gentleman. He was knocked onto the floor, and in a frenzie of motions the killer began to eat the victim! The lady escaped and went running into the dining quarters, one deck below. There she ran into Tina.

The time passed too quickly, for the shadow "being" followed into the dining room area. Frantic, the occupants were being targeted and eaten – for hunger? Or maybe for sport? Tina and the lady made their way to the kitchen, where they met Cheryl and Randy. Tina was in tears, as she explained what just happened. There was not much time. Tina feared that that they would be hunted very soon and effectively by this killer. Tina brought the group into a secret research lab. The lab was one part of a major experiment for "transport". There was no time to explain. The group entered the transport vessel and exited the underwater city, with one large flash of light!

The End (continued in chapter 2)

CHAPTER 2

TRANSPORT

The researchers made a way to the kitchen. The doors were locked and they found Randy with Tina and Cheryl. There was an immense level of fear in each set of eyes. Fear of the surrounding chaos. The researchers gathered around Tina, she knew the ship well and she was starting to share some of the grewsome events. They all listened carefully, as she whispered. The ship was locked down. There was no way to escape, to get back to the surface. Not now and perhaps never. One of the many experiments included the gathering of intelligence for "alien survivors". There were a few that were in a preserved state. The experiments were successful. About a year ago, they were able to revive a group of alien passengers. However, it was discovered that the anatomy and physiology of the aliens were not conducive to the world above. They were essentially trapped in the laboratory chambers, where they had been "revived". Randy stopped Tina. "Wait one minute, because Cheryl and I distinctly observed two non-human beings pass us, on the way out of the entry way!" Tina asked if they were positive? And they were! Odd, and Tina continued. This should not be, since the physiology could not buffer the internal body from the external environment. In humans, the blood flow through the body had more than just a "transport of oxygen and carbon dioxide" role. Yes, it was key and it was important to transport.... The internal tissues and organs and cells all needed fresh supply of oxygen. This was accomplished with the effective and efficient human circulatory system. The human blood consists of two major parts. An "iron" part and a part full of proteins (antibodies, white blood cells, immunological cells for protection). The iron is extremely efficient in binding the oxygen and the carbon dioxide. So, as the human lung brings in fresh oxygen, there is an exchange of carbon dioxide (blue blood) with fresh oxygen from the lungs (red blood). After the exchange, in the lungs, the fresh oxygen is quickly brought back into the heart via the pulmonary vein. The oxygen fresh blood enters the left atrium, where it is quickly moved into a very muscular left ventricle. The left human heart ventricle pumps, with great power, the fresh oxygen blood into the remaining parts of the human circulatory system.... the major arteries and smaller capillaries – where each tissue, organ and cell are bathed in fresh oxygen!The thing is, these aliens can not and do not have this type of effective circulation to survive outside of this ship! And the human blood has a "buffering effect" within the human body. It essentially keeps us in a state of balance. Where pH does not fluctuate to drastically. A drastic change in the blood chemistry pH would result in organ failure and certain death. The pH is carefully and constantly monitored by higher human organ systems, like the kidney and internal receptors of the internal arteries. The aliens do not have this evolutionary based protection... unless, a secret experiment enabled them to mimic our own internal biological and chemical systems! Randy and Cheryl both interrupted Tina. Good minds think alike! Randy paused and listened to Cheryl speak.... That's it! The aliens found a way to leave the ship, perhaps "blend in" as humans.... And now they are killing all the human passengers on the ship.... And once they finish with the murders, they will leave the ship and blend into the human population... above... and then what? There was an uncomfortable silence in the kitchen as they heard a banging sound and scream, just outside the locked kitchen door! The sound traveled away from the door and down the hallway.... Tina then continued. There is only one thing we can do. If we make our way to the seventh level of the ship, there is an experiment. The lab is called "the bend in time research project".

There, we have a chance to exit the ship! Randy interrupted, "wait, what does bend in time mean?" Again, an uncomfortable pause and silence.... as more screaming was heard just outside the kitchen door. When it was safe, Tina continued. Truth be told = I think it means transport to another place in time? Not sure, that wasn't my research project! Randy replied: "wonderful!".

There was a way to exit the kitchen, via ducts. They would silently make their way to the "bend in time research project lab". Cheryl and Randy held hands as they snaked their way through secret passages... ultimately, reaching the secret lab. They entered the lab and quickly locked the door.

Ship Level 7: bend in time research lab

Truth be told.... The transport was too easy. They found themselves in a deep wooded forest, in God's country. The transport may have led them away from the ship, they were no longer in the abyss of the Atlantic-ocean. The surroundings were ancient-like, too fresh. The plant life was enormous and the air was too clean, too fresh. Tina gathered the researchers and explained that this must just be the "path" needed for the next "jump". One researcher shrieked in terror: "jump to where!". The crew calmed the researcher. Cheryl offered a suggestion: let's camp the night, since it's getting late. Anyone knew how to start a good camp fire? .....So, there they were. A group of young researchers – lost in time and space, for the moment. The physiology fascinated Randy. As they set the camp, with a nice camp fire – they began to talk. Luckily, there was a "pro-active researcher" that was keen enough to think ahead. She brought a back pack full of food and water! Some basic essential supplies, like a lighter and a few flash lights. The lead assistant, Tina, shed an enormous amount of light on the situation. These "creatures", the aliens... they were not of this galaxy. The technology that was found in the ship was truly amazing. Out of this world technological advancements. Most of the gadgets were not even understandable. But, for the technology applications that were of immediate "practical application" ... well, that stuff was pretty cool!

Tina was a biologist by night and an explorer by day! She was not the only researcher that was aware of the "bend in time" research project. And she feared that they would be followed by one of the killers. So, they needed two guards for the night shift, while they rested. Two gentlemen eagerly volunteered for the posts. The sleeping arrangements were tight. They wanted to stay in a small circle, near the camp fire. Not too close to the heat, but close enough to scare off any animals. Randy had an interest in learning more about the physiology of the aliens. He asked Cheryl if it would be okay to sleep near Tina. And they did. They whispered through the night, but learned a great deal. Tina spoke first of their eating habits. The digestive system was so different from human digestion. The human digestion started the minute the food entered the mouth! An enzyme Amylase was efficiently released near the back-molar teeth. Sort of a secretion you could call it. The purpose of this amylase was to essentially start "breaking the food". Tina gently placed her hand on Randy's right forearm, then slid it to his leg. She smiled and asked if he wanted to hear more? Randy was truly fascinated with the discussion. He spent time as a biology student, learning the foundational concepts of "digestion". So, he was following Tina very well. He was also intrigued with how inviting her soft sparkling brown eyes were. They sang an unspoken melody to his heart, it seemed. Tina continued with the discussion. After the food is ingested, it follows the human esophagus. This long tube is a "transport" to the human stomach. And in the stomach, the food is essentially "stored". During storage of a "good meal" (let's call it), the stomach adds a very acidic environment. The acidity of the stomach further breaks the food down. Randy stopped Tina and asked what the acidy level was? She smiled. "you really are curious about the digestive process!" He smiled back. The stomach is incredibly acidic! Reaching a pH as low as 1.8 to 2.0! Very far from the neutral 7.0 pH level! In the human physiology, it is what happens next that is fascinating. The small intestine captures all the critical nutrients! The vitamins, the protein, the peptides, the amino acids all get "absorbed" through the small intestine. After absorption, the nutrients are transported via circulation throughout the body – to be used to sustain many cellular processes (like mitosis, and bathe existing cells, tissues, organs). After the small intestine there is further digestive processing in the large intestine and storage in the colon, where eventually the waste (non nutrients) are excreted.

The aliens have no such anatomy and digestive physiology. They seem to achieve the "nutrient absorption" through "biting". They have fangs that dig deep into their prey to absorb needed nutrients... Cheryl interrupted: "what are these things? Like, are they vampires?" ...They slept through the night and woke to a fresh jungle breeze. The researchers were ready to move forward. Tina advised that they needed to get to a trail that would ultimately bring them to the next "transport zone". Another researcher came walking from behind large trees and bushes. His name was Lewis. The American name. They weren't sure what the "Chinese name" for Lewis was. He was a senior level researcher, on the ship. He seemed distraught. Something had startled him. Lewis advised that they better come take a look. The researchers followed him into a deep wood area, where they found forests of indigenous bamboo. Among the bamboo were the largest trees they had ever seen! These trees would put the large California Red Woods to shame. Incredible density, circumference. And the height... who knew? Perhaps five hundred feet! Some of the low branches of these trees is where Lewis pointed to.... He gestured with his finger to his lip – to be very quiet. Above, hanging from some area tree branches were the most monster-like "bats" they had ever observed! They literally were the size of human beings, except very fury and dark! The researchers carefully left the wooded area to return to the camp. Lewis was arguing with Tina. Something was not right in this transport area. Lewis had been through this research transport, many times. There was something different this time. For one thing, the sky looked bleak. It was not bright, it seemed "grey". The air was fresh, but even the air seemed different to him. And what in the world was hanging from the large tree branches? ...

Tina asked if anyone had any weapons? Randy showed the group his collection of large pocket knives. Perfect for hunting.... Or protection from large vampire bats! He smirked with excitement. Tina smiled back, but most of the other researchers were not amused by his humor. Tina asked if he could keep the knives ready... just in case they would need them! He agreed. They started hiking across the jungle, together... taking turns for the 2nd position. Cheryl asked why the second position in the line was such a "fearing position". Tina said that it is the first position, the first person that will come across a large jungle snake... however, "survival 101" teaches that the person in the second position will be the one that will be 'bitten" by the snake, after it is startled! Cheryl grabbed Randy's hand and squeezed gently. The researchers continued their hike...

Tina found the research transport facility. Amongst the savage prehistoric like jungle, stood a large modernized looking building. Inside the building, it exhibited a similar ambience to the alien ship. Similar to the submerged alien ship, the transport facility had living quarters. A nice modern kitchen, loaded with plenty of food and snacks! And, within the central area – an entertainment room. They all "camped" there. First, finding a good movie to watch and second, arranging the furniture – so they could sleep comfortably on a fuzzy rug. The walls were paneled with cherry wood. The wall art and style was "antique-like". It offered an inviting feel. While eating, Tina asked if Randy and Cheryl could come with her to the transport lab. Within the lab, she advised that there was a problem. During lockdown (the murders on the submerged ocean ship) the transport to the surface was disabled. It was part of the very effective protocol. No in or out during the investigation. Another part of the protocol must be to also disable the lab projects. She was hoping that she could bypass the protocol. She could not. A long silence filled the room. Tina proposed that they return to the living quarters and talk to the others, to see what a good approach was. Before leaving the room, Randy inquired about the "aliens". What are these creatures? Are they usually good natured?

Tina was in deep thought. Then started to speak: the aliens are different. The anatomy and physiology is different from humans. Although, they are surprisingly similar in appearance to us. Tina thought out loud, wondering if they were able to change their appearance. There was so much they did not know. They were still in the process of learning about the ship, the technology found on the ship and some of the aliens. For example, the muscles and how the movement of these creatures differed from humans. In the human physiology, the control of muscle movement was fascinating.... There was an incredible amount of "signaling" .... Electrical signals! So quick that it would literally blow your mind! Randy and Cheryl listened to Tina, as they pulled up chairs to sit.... The neurons, the receptors, the relay systems, the processing into the central nervous system and back out to the human muscles was quick! Split second decisions.... And just like that, the electrical signal snapped along "axons" within the human body. It was not just electrical signaling though. There was more! There were "spaces" where the electrical signals stopped and "chemical messengers" took over. And in those areas, things like acetylcholine was released and would travel to other areas, which ultimately led to "muscle contraction"! The aliens did not have these systems in their physiology. And when they walked, even though they resembled the human being, they did not walk the same! What Tina feared the most, was the perceived lack of "soul". It seemed to be missing. It was a curious thing. Not that we humans could medically pinpoint the soul. However, people knew the "good soul" when they were in his or her presence! It was sort of a feeling. Looking deep into the eyes helped locate a human soul – sometimes.

They decided to leave and join the others. Tina did not want to break the bad news to the group tonight. She would wait till the next morning. Cheryl and Randy slept together, cuddled. The lights were dimmed and they fell asleep. Randy woke in the middle of the night with a feeling that they were being watched. In the distant, dark hallway.... He could see a dark shadowy figure – in the shape of a black cat.... The next day, Randy woke and brewed a fresh pot of coffee. It was a good way to start any day. Even if the day was in a "transport forest"! Tina was the first of the researchers to wake. She followed the fresh coffee bean aroma. Tina met Randy in the kitchen. She was dressed in very revealing pajamas! Randy was finding it difficult not to stare. He was a gentleman and he did not want to stare. The invisible pheromones that were released had other plans for him. It was as if a hand was reaching out and effectively redirecting his attention to her soft skin. They were going to be staying in the transport facility for at least a few days. Tina wanted to try a few things – and hopefully the transporter would "activate". They were content with the facility. It had food, supplies, a shower, clean clothes. Tina asked Randy if he could help her find the shower. They looked over at the group sleeping... and left for the second floor. Just on top of the stair well was a hallway that led to sleeping quarters and showers. Right outside the shower room was a nice room that had a couch and a large cushioned chair. The chair could be considered a "love couch", but was probably just an over sized chair. As they walked into the room, Tina tripped and fell into Randy... they landed, together, on the large chair....

The pheromones engulfed Tina and Randy. Tina's vanilla scent and taste were absorbed into Randy. She grabbed Randy below the waist and continued for quite a while... In fact, Tina was thinking that the time that had passed could be shared doing some other things... since he was able to "last and show pretty good endurance" .... another time, they would continue... for now, Tina kissed Randy and left to shower. He returned to the kitchen to taste another fresh cup of coffee...

It was noon. The researchers were waiting for Lewis to return. He had left almost 2 hours ago to collect fresh wood, for a fire. Lewis and his colleague were adventurous and strong. The researchers were beginning to worry about them. Lewis just then opened the door, with a small bundle of kindling wood and deep gashes through his blood-soaked skin! He said: "we have a problem". His friend followed just behind him with large wood for the fire place. They started the fire in the wood burning space, located within the antique styled living room. As a medical student tended to their wounds, they all sat around the warm fire place to listen to Lewis. He had been attacked viciously by what appeared to be a dark black cat! The cat did not kill him and he thinks that there was a reason for that. As Lewis left the dark forest, he could see the cat change shape. The cat was in the form of an alien! And it or him or her.... Left with what appeared to be six-foot fury vampire bats. Where they were headed to, he had no idea. The researchers cringed and one broke down in despair. She sobbed saying that they would never make it out of the transport forest. And perhaps she was correct. Lewis continued with his "theory". Even Tina was frightened. She gently moved closer to Randy and placed her hand on his leg. Lewis believed that the cat or let's say "alien" was heading to the other side of the jungle. There, he would find a master control facility. And there the transport back to the ocean ship could take place. And perhaps transport to the surface too... he really was not completely familiar with the bend in time research technology. The transport may even bring them to other worlds, he just did not know. And that is why the 5000+ researchers were on board the ocean ship. To learn more of the advanced alien technologies. His fear now, though – was that most (if not all) of the researchers on board the ship wasmurdered. And the group that survived, that had made it to the transport forest... would also be targeted by the aliens. It seemed to him that the aliens found a way to adapt to the surface environment and they wanted to "blend in" to the surface. In order to do this, they would have to eliminate all researchers that were aware of their existence. The researchers were convinced that this "theory" was most likely very true. Especially since they could still hear the violent murders that occurred on board the ship, just prior to escaping... the sounds were etched in their memories.... Randy asked Lewis: "How do we kill these sons of bitches?" ...

Lewis was familiar with the alien's anatomy and physiology. Even he admitted that the advancement of these creatures was too much to comprehend. It seemed that these aliens were more of what a human would call "supernatural". Mostly, just because they did not understand how these aliens functioned. What Lewis did know, was that they were vicious – when provoked or when they were "in attack mode". The aliens needed blood, the components of blood to keep a life balance. Sort of like a vampire. They were fast, they had an ability to mimic the body of a human. The mimic was similar to the human anatomy, but not perfect. Looking closely into the eyes, the alien exhibited a "cat-like" glow. Sort of a shimmer of light. And the nose bridge did not have the same anatomical orientation. Their walk differed from humans. Although, the aliens found ways to effectively blend in to the human population – even with these differences. Lewis continued... there were other things that he suspected, but could not prove. He thought that there was a possibility for these aliens to enter the human body – and take control of the human body. Randy said: "great". So, just about every researcher on the ship has been murdered....and the aliens were most likely making their way to the surface. To take over the world? Lewis agreed. And continued... this is a very real possibility. They needed to get over to the other edge of the forest and take out the "aliens". At least, that was the first part of the plan!It's not like the group was just going to leave and start travel. In search for super strong aliens to kill! Tina wanted to try and get the transport module working. The group agreed and hoped that she would be able to get it operating properly. Lewis thought that he could also help her take a look at the module. While they were pretty much stuck where they were (for the time being) – the group decided to take a walk around the surrounding facility. Lewis thought he had seen a shed. And if there was a shed, perhaps it held useful supplies. Perhaps, there would be "weapons" they could use against the aliens they would soon encounter. The forest was deep, containing pine trees and also populations of large redwood trees. The trees reached enormous heights – similar to incredible skyscrapers found in large cities. Only not comprised of strong steel. The trees were wood, a living system….Cheryl and Randy followed the researchers into the living area to relax. They found some food for dinner and enjoyed a quiet evening near the living room fire. Tina left to look at the transport room. Lewis was planning to meet her up in the transport room. He wanted to search the shed for weapons, with his colleague. It was getting darker as Lewis walked toward the shed. His friend pointed out that there really was no clear "sunshine". It had seemed dark most of the day! The flashlights came in handy.... Inside the shed, it was more like a large pharmaceutical company "warehouse"! As far as the eye could see... were large, tall shelves – stocked with supplies. And there were plenty of weapons! Not high-tech stuff. But, that was okay with Lewis. He found shot guns, hand guns, large blades! Good enough to take care of evil dwelling aliens! They were sort of relieved that they did not stumble upon sophisticated, space aged laser beamed weapons. They would not know how to use the gear! The lighting absolutely sucked in this warehouse. They were walking around looking for a light switch.... Lewis asked his friend if he heard something rustling in the distance....

Approaching the dark, very tall fury vampire bat was quick. They had not seen the sucker! But, he was there. It was the glowing eyes that gave up his position. The large creature swiftly and effectively crunched its long fangs into the side of Lewis' skull. The blunt force killed him instantly. His friend turned to run, and fell into another bat....Cheryl snuggled in close with Randy, on the couch. It was a scene right out of the "Casablanca movie". A feeling that words could never describe accurately. A picture that could at least reach the "surface of extreme happiness, greater than extreme happiness.... a euphoria....". The fire place was nice. It complemented the antique style room. Cheryl complemented Randy. He lost her once before, and he was not going to lose her again. He thought how stupid he had been to stray.... The front door slammed open and one of the researchers stumbled in. He fell on the floor, a bloody mess... he mumbled something about bats before slipping into a coma... and ultimately dying! There were screams, as one of the bats entered the living room area...

Randy gently grabbed Cheryl and calmly asked if she still had her bag? She did and immediately knew what he was driving at. Randy had asked her to keep a collection of military grade knives, for him. Randy started to quietly whisper, as he readied the selected blades. Turn, and do not look back... quickly make your way to the transport room, where Tina is. Now! Randy gently pressed his lips onto her tear soaked cheek.... And instantly, they were apart! There was a lot of spilled blood as Randy made his way across the room. In his mind it was complex, yet simple. Accuracy and Precision ... [think of the anatomy and physiology, wait...these beasts have different composition!] The blade was sharp, and would cut deep. He had two! Trying not to think of the murdered researchers, he approached this tall beast. The first weapon was released and landed in the "shoulder area". Not to inflict a kill, but more to distract the creature. The vampire turned and stumbled forward, bending over - in the direction of the sliced shoulder.... And Randy continued with a final blow, using the other sharp knife. Accurately and precisely the weapon pierced the rear neck region. This was just a theory, and a good one at that! There was a neural network collection in the back, upper neck region [he learned this from Tina's lectures! A neural network that was similar to the human central nervous system].

The creature was "still", and Randy moved away quickly... only to be viciously attacked by what looked like a black cat! The cat sank its sharp teeth and claws into Randy's upper leg – deep into his quad muscles! Before he had time to react, the cat was gone – almost disappearing through the open front door.... He thought of helping the wounded researchers, but there were none. The ones attacked, were killed instantly. The remaining researchers were in a state of shock. He closed and locked the front door, hoping that what-ever was outside would leave (for now). Randy suggested that the other researchers walk with him, up to where Tina and Cheryl were. They slowly and cautiously made their way to the transport room. Cheryl ran over to Randy and hugged him – with tears rolling down her cheeks. He was happy to be alive, lucky to be alive... They closed and locked the transport room door. Tina found a first aid kit and helped clean the deep gashes of Randy's leg. The kit had some sterile gauze that she used to cover the cleaned cuts. Randy thanked Tina for being gentle. The peroxide she used, immediately killed any foreign disease-causing bugs! He noticed an extreme amount of white bubbling, similar to the froth found on rough ocean beaches. This was a good indicator for the peroxide destroying the bacteria present in the wound. They all agreed to spend the night in the transport room. Tina would try to figure out a way to activate the transport technology. The others would rest for the night.

It was a quiet night. Randy felt his leg, and was relieved that it was starting to feel somewhat "healthy". Tina was frustrated that the transport was still in an "inactive state". There was a small group that remained. Eight in total. Randy proposed that they take action, immediately. Not that he was thrilled with his "plan". But, what choice did they have? To wait and be murdered by tall bat looking aliens and a crazy black cat. A black cat that likes to sink its razor-sharp teeth into human flesh! No, they were first going to collect supplies and weapons. Then, they would travel through the "jungle" during the day. The theory was that the creatures were nocturnal. Hopefully, the bats would be asleep during the day – as the researchers traveled through the uncharted territory. In the evenings, the group would hide out.

There was one objection to the plan. Tina and one researcher decided that it would be best to stay back. It was important for Tina to get the transporter to activate. It was the only way to get back to the surface, above the ocean. Or, perhaps, the transport would bring them to another time or place. Randy asked if Cheryl could join the two. She refused and grabbed his arm. They said their good byes to Tina. It was day-time, and they needed to start the trip. Inside the shed, the researchers grabbed camping gear. The weapons and ammo were also selected. The jungle was filled with large rain-forest like trees….Not your typical stroll through a forest. It seemed more mysterious to the group of researchers. The forest had patches of light, some sort of a natural light source. They wondered if that truly was a sun beam breaching the tree canopy, above. After a long day hike through an ever-inclined forest floor… the researchers stopped near what seemed to be a natural lake. It was getting late. They planned to set up camp, right next to the lake.

Cheryl and another lady researcher proposed that they take a swim in the lake. After camp was ready, a few stayed to start a small camp fire... and prepare dinner. The rest ventured into the lake. It was a good day for a swim. The group submerged into the cool lake water, wearing the 'bare essentials".

The surroundings were similar to the mountainous terrain of the Adirondack territory, upstate New York. The lake water felt cool on Randy and Cheryl's skin. It was refreshing. The group swam for awhile and enjoyed the time together. The lake stretched as far as the eye could see. And after that, it seemed to continue.... Randy noticed movement at the other end of the lake. The natural current was there, and a cool breeze brought refreshing air their way. There was also something swimming toward the group, very rapidly. And as this "creature" breached the lake water surface, a "dolphin" appeared. Cheryl reached out to the dolphin and felt its nose…. The beast was friendly. The beast was cute. As the dolphin cut gracefully through the waters, it disappeared. In the distance, the sky darkened. The air got noticeably colder. They could see their breath as it dispersed…. The group left the lake water. Most of the group. Except for two. Randy and Cheryl heard a loud scream. Something appeared at the end of the lake. It rapidly attacked, moving forward toward the dolphin. After consuming the dolphin, this ugly creature moved faster. Too fast to even react. The two researchers attempted to leave the lake water. It was too late…..they were instantly attacked!

The lake water turned a dark red-black color, as two bodies were taken violently into the distance....

The group of researchers (what was left of the group) huddled around the camp fire. Whatever was in the lake had left... for now. One suggested that they keep a watch, while the others rested. Just in case the lake monster returned. Although, they doubted that the monster would return. The creature had enough dolphin meat and human flesh to eat!They did not know much about this "research experiment", the "bend in time project". It was odd to them. The fact that they found themselves in what was called a "transport forest". One of the researchers started to explain what she knew of the alien technology. It was out of this world stuff. Not fully understood, but over the months they were convinced that the transport technology opened up into another "hidden dimension". The dimension was sort of a back drop from the reality that most humans were accustomed too. And there they were, in this "other dimension". They did not know where the transport forest would ultimately bring the group to? For now, that was low on the list of priorities! The top priority was to track down a crazy black cat with sharp claws. And to track down tall vampire bat monsters. Randy left the group to climb one of the largest forest trees. At the top of the tree, he could see a dark mountain in the distance....

Cheryl followed and called up to Randy. She was at the base of the tree, looking upward. She could not see Randy, he had climbed high up into the tree.... Randy heard his name, and started to carefully descend the trunk. At the bottom of the tree, Randy and Cheryl found a nice place to sit. They leaned against the forest wood, together. The forest was mysterious and Randy mentioned what he observed in the distance. At that moment in time, the challenges did not matter. What mattered were the hugs they shared, together. They relaxed, listening to the breeze move through the forest leaves. The ground was filled with pine needles and large oak tree leaves. There was a strong scent of pine and wood.... It was getting dark, they were concerned about what would happen during the night... The vampire aliens (if that is what they were) would be around. Cheryl interrupted Randy. "did you see that?" He looked in the distance. There were large leaves in brush moving... Randy opened one of his military grade knives and walked cautiously ahead.... At the site of a large bush, they saw a group of teenagers, hiding within the deep forest! They were frightened, and Randy quickly hid his knife. "Come out, its okay – we are researchers from the ship...". There was a group of five teenage girls. The "leader of the group" introduced herself: "I am Madison". Randy and Cheryl welcomed the group to their campsite. Madison explained that they were kids of other researchers, from the ship. The physics department experimentation level. When the aliens murdered the ship researchers, their parents directed them to go to the research lab. They were familiar with the transport module, after all they were prodigy of physicists! Their family advised to come here and hide in the forest until it was safe. Then to transport to the surface! …. The group fascinated Randy and Cheryl. They had left just when the murders started… They were hiding in the forest. Hiding from the indigenous dangers… hiding from the aliens. They planned to wait one week, then they would transport back to the surface….

It was getting late. The sky was getting dark, and the teenagers advised Cheryl to get the group. All the researchers, including the pack of teenagers were alarmed at how fast the sky darkened. The vampire people were nocturnal. They surely would be out at night, ready for feeding. Randy hoped that Tina was okay. He hoped that she made some progress with getting the transport module to "activate". The group gravitated toward Madison. They followed her to a large "red wood tree". These trees were amazing, something from pre-historic times! At the base of the large red wood tree, an entrance opened! They all entered quickly, leaving the darkness behind. The tree entrance closed, with a secure hissing sound. There must be a hydraulic mechanism that was used to open and close the front door! Inside the large tree, was a passageway. The passage was lit dimly with a fluorescent light. As they moved forward, a staircase descended into an underground bunker.

Cheryl asked how they knew of this underground place. The teenagers smiled and advised that their parents were responsible for this research project. They practically were raised in this forest! Over the many years of research, the teenagers would come to this very place to learn more about the technology. And, to this day, they did not fully comprehend how all the technology functioned! It was so advanced. It was from another world. The "transport forest" was one link in the technology. Inside the chamber, where Tina was located – the shuttle (in an activated state) would propel the group to the surface. However, there were many mysteries – unexplained mysteries – in the forest...The bunker had some basic comforts of home. A bathroom, shower, a sleeping area... a kitchen with food! A television to watch some movies.... They would spend the night in this underground bunker, safe from the surrounding evil. It was cozy, as the group gravitated to the sleeping area. They were tired from traveling through the forest. As they rested, Madison spoke with some other teenagers.... Randy and Cheryl listened. The bend in time research project was controlled by a central station. The station was a facility that they needed to get to. Inside the facility were activation switches – which would initiate the transport manual, near Tina (located clear across the length of the forest). Cheryl asked where the central station was located? The teenagers said "at the top of the mountain". There was an old rail station inside the forest. Iron tracks that held some vehicles. After a good night's rest, the group planned to leave the underground bunker and find the rail vehicles. The rails would guide them to the base of the large mountain. They discussed their plan for "climbing" the mountain. It was no ordinary mountain. It would not be easy to get to the top. Along the way, the mountain would "change" and they would find themselves in different places, in different times... challenged with evil... (hence the "bend in time research project" technology). It was physics! The teenagers laughed. They were not geeks. In fact, they were pretty cool, carefree souls... typical teenager types! With good senses of humor, with attitudes, with a zest for life! Madison spoke of physics being more than what people thought of when they heard the word "physics". The science encompassed many topics. Everything from the study of "light", and all its light properties... the transfer of heat, thermodynamics, architecture and electrical current movement... In this place, especially at the top of the mountain, the understanding of electrical circuits would prove helpful...!

The next day came fast. The group left the facility and found the rails. They traveled along the rails in two separate cars. Within what seemed to be approximately one hour – they were at the base of the dark looking mountain. They began the climb... this structure would test the group of researchers. They would need to stick together and endure the challenges. The mountain was no ordinary mountain. The structure would change abruptly...to another place and time.... and they would need to find a way to work through the evil that would surely attack them! As they climbed, the mountain did in fact change shape. Although it was early morning when they had arrived at the base of the mountain.... They were now in the middle of a large ocean! They found themselves on board a large military ship. The ship was rocking and rolling in rough ocean water. They heard the crew in the distance... it was a hurricane and the ship was trapped in turbulent seas. The group quickly entered the ship to get away from the fierce weather.

They found shelter in the interior part of the ship. The doors were closed shut, and secure to the outside weather elements. The violent waves crashed relentlessly against the hull of the ship. The turbulent seas rocked the ship from side to side. It was something fierce. It was something undescribed with mere words... After some time, the seas were calm. The storm had passed. Inside the ship, it was dark – with the exception of dim "red lights". The lights were located along the interior passageways... The ship literally was a floating city. However, something did not seem right. The ship seemed "empty of personnel". As the team of researchers made their way to the outside flight deck, they noticed a large vampire bat in the ships bridge. The area of the ship was located topside. The highest point on the ship. Where the ships movements were directed.... There stood a six to seven-foot tall, dark entity. A vampire person. An alien? Perhaps just pure evil. They would need to kill this beast in order to proceed to the next level of the mountain. Randy pulled his military grade, knives from a backpack. The knives were sharp, and he had managed to take one of these evil entities out (back in the jungle facility, where Tina was currently waiting…) and he would do it again… a slice to the shoulder to distract, a slice to the neural network. Located just behind the neck…

The bend in time project was odd to the group. As they made their way to the ship's bridge, they noticed "accuracy and precision" drills being performed. Large steel ICBMs (the ships fire power) were being fired into the distant ocean horizon. The flight deck opened to propel these large ICBMs (intercontinental ballistic missiles), propel upward and with great force. What was most disturbing was the vampires grin. Standing tall, overlooking the precision of the weapons – the vampire continued to direct the drills.... Which was good for the researchers... the vampire did not even see Randy approach, attack and end his existence. Ironically, the blade was directed with such precision and accuracy, that the vampire dropped ---- instantly, onto the cold hard ship's steel floor. A dark mist appeared, and carried the surrounding ocean away. The researchers were left. And the mountain reappeared. They continued to climb....At the top of the mountain, a group of vampires were observed. The leader seemed to be the vicious black cat! Congregated around an electrical box – were the group of evil players. Randy gestured with his shiny, sharp knife. And with a subtle grin, he approached the evil group. Sheer luck, sheer will – the evil was removed. With precision, with accuracy. The teenagers looked in aww! Then asked if they could hold his military grade knife. They were momentarily safe, at the top of the dark mountain. What was odd though, was the fact that the cat had disappeared! Randy was not sure where the cat could have disappeared too? It was a mountain and there weren't too many places to hide. At least, not at the top of the mountain. Perhaps, the cat quickly and silently made its way back down the mountain side?

Madison opened the electrical box and started thinking... The circuitry was complex. But, no match for the young physicist. After about five minutes, the green lights were all lit. And she smiled. They were ready to travel back to the facility, where Tina was.... Familiarity with the jungle helped the group travel quickly and within a short period of time, they were back with Tina. It was nice to be back "home" (sort of a home). The facility provided shelter, food and a nice fire place to rest warm up too. They rested after eating. Tina met Madison and the transport module was ready to bring the group to their final destination...They waited a day to travel. The group was tired and just wanted to rest. Early, the next morning the group travelled back to the surface. Not to the ship, but right back to the house along side the raging river... In a small New Jersey town, where once agent orange was manufactured for a war...

The End (continued in chapter 3)

CHAPTER 3

Randy woke to a blurred vision. He could feel Cheryl gently rubbing his cheek. Then, he could hear her calm voice: "are you okay?". His vision became clearer. Randy was on the floor, located next to the bookshelf. The room was dimly lit with light. And at the other side of the room was the staircase that had led them into this area. Randy asked what had happened? Cheryl smiled.

She said that they were hiding behind the bookcase, thinking that people were walking by... when the bookcase fell over onto them! [Randy hit his head, and was knocked unconscious! Cheryl was ready to leave to get help. A good hour had passed and she was worried that Randy would not wake up. And just then, when she was ready to leave for help.... Randy woke up! He asked her about the research ship, the jungle, the pack of teengers...] Cheryl looked at him, with a face of confusion. Cheryl said: "what are you talking about?". You were asleep, there is no ship, no teenagers, no forest...!

They walked up the staircase, through the hole in the floor and eventually out of the abandoned house. The path from the house to the river was covered with debris. Tree leaves and dust.... The train ride back to Long Island was quiet. They passed through New Jersey, into Manhattan. Boarded the "Long Island Train" in Penn Station. The Long Island train ride was approximately and hour. The small train station, located in Medford Long Island was nice to see. A familiar place. Cheryl and Randy left the stopped train, descended the steps of the rail road station, and began to walk back to their modest home. They passed a carvel, stopped to get ice cream, then continue to walk.... The ice cream was good! It was a Saturday evening and they were exhausted. Normally they might order Chinese take-out food for dinner. But, tonight they decided to shower, cook something from home and relax in the living room. Randy started the coal/wood burning stove. They relaxed by the warm, cozy fire place. As they listened to music and drank dry white wine – Randy recalled a similar setting. He asked Cheryl if she remembered snuggling in the forest facility? In the facility, where a nice fire place lit the elegant antique style room. She giggled and then smirked at him.

A few weeks went by. Randy continued his research project... with one exception. The "agent orange facility" was closed by the government! The company advised him to continue research on the samples he had previously taken. The samples were protected in cold storage. And he had plenty of agent orange river bank samples to still go through.... What was curious to him, was that the government closed the distant field facility down. He wondered why they would do that? Randy continued riding the train, back and forth between

Medford Long Island and the northern New Jersey mountains. He liked the trip. It was quiet, it gave him some time to rest. And it bypassed the rush hour car traffic!

One particular night upon arriving home, Cheryl was showering. He noticed a "red light". She had bought a heating lamp. Randy relaxed on the bed and started watching television, when he was startled by the presence of a "black cat"! The thing nearly scared him to death! It purred - he pet the beast. Within seconds, the purr turned into a growl and Randy found a deep slash mark in his hand! The cat had clawed him, then ran out of the room.... Cheryl came out of the shower and explained to Randy that they had a new animal, a kitty cat! He showed her what the beast had just done to him.... She then quickly grabbed the first aid kit from the bath room and taped up his wound. They snuggled on the bed and shared love and affection. Cheryl seemed more energetic these days, full of life, full of something.... Her hair seemed very shiny.... and Randy could swear that he saw her eyes glow in the dark! It had been a tough few-weeks... Randy was still recovering from his book case accident. His research field area was "quarantined". And as he traveled, he heard odd news reporting of strange happenings in the eastern Long Island suburbs (murders....). He wondered if there could be a link between what he thought he experienced (deep in the ocean abyss, deep in the transport forest....) to what was now happening in the suburbs....? And what was up with this black cat?

The End.